We praise You, Lord, for Brother Fire,
through whom You light the night.
He is beautiful, playful, robust and strong.

We praise You, Lord, for Sister Earth,
who sustains us
with her fruits, colored flowers, and herbs.

We praise You, Lord, for those who pardon,
for love of You bear sickness and trial.
Blessed are those who endure in peace,
by You Most High, they will be crowned.

We praise You, Lord, for Sister Death,
From whom no living thing can escape.
Woe to those who die in their sins!
Happy those She finds doing Your will!
No second death can do them harm.

We praise and bless You, Lord, and give You
thanks, and serve You in all humility.

Saint Francis of Assisi

Saint Francis and the Wolf

Saint Francis and the Wolf

by Jane Langton

illustrated by Ilse Plume

DAVID R. GODINE · Publisher · Boston

First published in 2007 by
D A V I D R . G O D I N E · *Publisher*
Post Office Box 450
Jaffrey, New Hampshire 03452
www.godine.com

LIBRARY OF CONGRESS CATALOGING-IN-PUBLICATION DATA
Langton, Jane.
Saint Francis and the wolf / by Jane Langton ; illustrations by Ilse Plume.—
1st ed.
p.   cm.
Summary: An old and hungry wolf terrorizes the townspeople of Gubbio
until Saint Francis shows the villagers how to live peacefully with the wolf.
ISBN-13: 978-1-56792-320-9 (hardcover)
ISBN-10: 1-56792-320-8 (hardcover)
1. Francis, of Assisi, Saint, 1182–1226—Legends. [1. Francis, of Assisi,
Saint, 1182–1226—Legends. 2. Wolves—Folklore. 3. Folklore—Italy.]
I. Plume, Ilse, ill. II. Title.
PZ8.1.L27Sai 2007
398.2—dc22
[E]

FIRST EDITION
Printed in China

This book is dedicated to Sister Mary Francis Hone, O.S.C.,
of the Convent of Poor Clares in Jamaica Plain, Massachusetts,
to Brother Bernardo Francesco Maria Gianni, O.S.B.,
of the Benedictine Order of San Miniato al Monte in Florence,
to the Sisters of Santa Elisabetta in Florence,
and to the Reverend Dace Zusmanis,
of the Latvian Lutheran Church of America.

Once a long time ago a great wolf prowled around the town of Gubbio, clawing at the gates by day and howling below the wall by night.

The people of Gubbio were frightened. They stared out their windows at the wolf and kept their children indoors.

"Let us out," cried the children. "We want to play in the fields."

"No, no," cried the mothers and fathers. "The wolf will gobble you up."

*A*t last they locked the city gate against the wolf. But then everyone was afraid to go outside the city wall.

The farmer could not harvest his grain. Therefore the miller had no grain to grind into flour. And the baker had no flour to bake into bread.

All the people were starving. The animals, too, had nothing to eat. A hungry dog chased a hungry cat. The cat scrambled up on the roof and looked down greedily at the hungry hen. "Oh, no!" cried the miller's wife, when the hungry goat ate all the flowers in her garden.

*B*ut the wolf was hungry too. It licked its chops, dreaming of fat sheep.

Not far away lived a joyful friar named Brother Francis, who loved the poor people of Assisi so much that he gave them everything he had. Thankfully they called him *il Poverello*, "the little poor man of Assisi."

Brother Francis also loved the humble beasts of the farmyard and the wild creatures of the forest. Even the birds, people said, gathered around him to sing.

*B*ut when Brother Francis heard about the wolf, he hurried to Gubbio.

"Don't be afraid," he told the people. "I will speak to the wolf."

"No, no," cried the farmer. "It is too dangerous, blessed one." But then he thought about the uncut grain in his field and fell silent.

"You must not go," cried the miller, but he remembered his silent grindstone and said no more.

"The wolf will eat you up," warned the baker's wife, holding her baby close in her arms. But the baker thought of his empty oven and said nothing.

*D*on't worry," said Brother Francis as he opened the city gate and went out to look for the wolf. "I am not afraid."

All the people of Gubbio ran to the city wall to see what would happen to Brother Francis. Would he kill the wolf? Would the wolf eat him up?

The baker shook his head and whispered, "He is a fool."

"No, no," cried the miller, "he is a saint."

But the farmer murmured sadly, "Fool or saint, he will surely die."

veryone watched fearfully as Brother Francis walked calmly across the valley to the little church in the field, the Chiesa della Vittorina. There he waited, looking left and right for the wolf.

He did not have to wait long.

"Watch out, Brother Francis," cried the farmer, pointing with a trembling finger. "There's the wolf!"

The miller groaned and covered his eyes.

The baker's wife wept because the teeth of the wolf were like daggers. She screamed, "Run, blessed one!"

*B*ut Brother Francis did not run.

When the wolf rushed at him and opened its terrible jaws, Brother Francis stood still and held out his hand.

"Come here, Brother Wolf," he said softly.

At once, the wolf stopped in its tracks. As gently as a lamb, it came to Brother Francis and bowed its shaggy head.

*B*rother Wolf," said Brother Francis, "you have frightened the people of Gubbio. You have become their enemy."

The wolf put its tail between its legs as if it were ashamed.

ow, Brother Wolf," said Brother Francis, "there must be peace between you and these good people. If you promise to do them no harm, they will feed you as long as you live."

The wolf wagged its tail.

"Do you promise, Brother Wolf?" said Brother Francis.

The wolf lifted its paw and laid it gently in the hand of Brother Francis. That was its promise.

*W*atching from the city wall, the people of Gubbio rejoiced. Church bells rang, and there was dancing in the street. The children laughed, the dogs barked, the cat came down from the rooftop, the rooster crowed, the hen cackled and laid an egg, and the goat licked the petals caught in its beard.

*J*oyfully the people of Gubbio thanked the little poor man of Assisi for setting them free from the bloodthirsty jaws of the wolf.

Brother Francis blessed them and went away.

At last the farmers could reap the grain in their fields.

Once again the grindstone of the miller thundered and ground the grain into flour, and at last the baker fired up his oven and baked the flour into bread.

Faithfully the wolf kept its promise to Brother Francis, and so did the people of Gubbio.

From that day on, the wolf was treated as a citizen of the town. It went in and out of the houses to play with the children and to be petted and fed.

But after two years of friendship between the people of Gubbio and the wild creature of the forest, Brother Wolf died of old age. Everyone mourned.

His gentle presence in Gubbio had been a reminder of the goodness in all living things.

The Life of Saint Francis of Assisi

The order of Franciscan monks was founded eight hundred years ago in a small town in Italy.

The founder was born in Assisi in 1182. After a swashbuckling life as the son of a rich merchant, Francis Bernardone was inspired to dress in rags and give away to the poor all that he had.

Dismayed, his father disowned him, but Francis was content to live in poverty. He felt a special call to preach, to cure the sick, to give as freely as he had received, and to carry neither gold nor silver.

Soon he had many followers. Gathering them into a monastic order, he urged them "never to own anything under the sun, and to have no other inheritance but begging."

These words sound harsh to us, and yet the spirit of Brother Francis was joyful. He rejoiced especially in a love for the natural world.

In his famous "Canticle of the Sun," he gave thanks for Sister Moon and Brother Sun, for Sister Water and Brother Wind, and even for Our Sister, the Death of the Body.

Brother Francis was only forty-four years old when Sister Death came for him. Two years later he was canonized by Pope Gregory IX as Saint Francis of Assisi.

A Note on the Type

SAINT FRANCIS AND THE WOLF *has been set in Adobe's Brioso Pro, a type designed by Robert Slimbach. Based on humanist calligraphic hands of the Renaissance, Brioso's letterforms are derived from a complex mixture of classical Roman capitals and Carolingian minuscules. Slimbach's design includes a range of ligatures, swashes, and alternate characters that elegantly replicate the effect of a broad-nibbed pen on paper. Unlike most calligraphic faces, Brioso has both a roman and an italic, a feature that makes it especially adaptable, and allows for a livelier page than a more conventional italic type.*

DESIGN AND COMPOSITION BY CARL W. SCARBROUGH